Mrs. Weddington's Yard

David R. Beshears

Greybeard Publishing
Washington State

Greybeard Publishing
P.O. Box 480
McCleary, WA 98557-0480

ISBN 978-1-947231-62-7 (paperback edition)

Mrs. Weddington's Yard

Chapter One

A large raven was perched on a slender branch high in the tree, was quietly observing the early-morning goings-on in the nearby backyard below. This was one of four regular stops that he would make on his daily morning explore of the neighborhood.

His name was Reggie.

He didn't know that his name was Reggie, of course. He didn't know that he had a name, though it was clearly understood that he had an identity, this by which the handful of fellow ravens, and more than a few of the neighborhood crows, knew him.

But not a name.

Reggie was a good name. It was the name given to him by The Woman.

The Woman cared for the yard below; the yard and the menagerie of animals that occupied the yard, all safely enclosed within a high wooden fence. The Woman's name was Mrs. Alvina Weddington, though Reggie didn't know that. To Reggie, her identity was The Woman. That was how he knew her.

There had at one time also been The Man. Reggie remembered him. The Woman and The Man had been the creators of the yard, a labyrinth of narrow winding paths, two small ponds, a number of shrubs and small trees. Several storage sheds were clustered together within one of the small clearings, and along the paths were a number of small habitats for the animals, each of the dwellings designed to meet the specific needs of the animals that dwelt within each.

There were pygmy goats, chickens, a mama pig and her babies, ducks and rabbits, a turkey and an elderly goose.

At the moment, Reggie was watching The Tortoise. The tortoise's name was Jeremiah, though Reggie didn't know that. For Reggie, its identity was The Tortoise.

Just now, Jeremiah the Tortoise was settled before the back porch of The Woman's dwelling. He was watching the back door, had been doing so since well before Reggie had arrived at this first stop along his morning explore.

Reggie was slightly curious at this.

By this time in the morning The Woman should have come out of her dwelling and should have been busily going about her own morning activity, which was feeding and carrying for the menagerie of animals that resided within the yard.

But she had yet to come out of her dwelling.

And so Reggie wondered. Might there be a connection? Was there a connection between The Woman not present and The Tortoise silently standing watch?

Ah, well.

Reggie slowly stretched one wing, then the other.

Time to move on to the second stop along his morning explore.

Jeremiah was the name given the tortoise by Mother, and Mother was the true and proper name of The Woman. Jeremiah sat silent, unmoving, eyes focused on the back door of Mother's dwelling.

Something was wrong.

Something was very wrong.

Jeremiah could feel it. He had a sense for this sort of thing.

A turkey came proudly strutting up and stood tall beside Jeremiah. The turkey, Owen by name, said nothing for several long moments, and carefully studied the back door of Mother's dwelling.

This was the second day.

Mother hadn't come out to tend to her children the day before, and had yet to come out this morning.

This was not how it was supposed to be.

"I don't like this, Jeremiah," said Owen. "I don't like it. Not one little bit."

"Nor I, Owen," said Jeremiah, his voice low and deep. He thought of expanding on his concern, but what was the point?

Owen and Jeremiah again both fell silent, each watching the back door from which Mother had emerged each and every morning, and most days several additional times throughout the day.

Owen and Jeremiah each silently willed for the door to open.

It remained closed.

Owen looked back behind them then, to the yard, their home.

Owen was a very important turkey and he must not shirk his duty. The yard was counting on him.

The morning rounds was but one of several rounds that he made each and every day.

Such was Owen's duty, his responsibility.

Whatever else, Owen would not let down the residents of the yard.

Duty above all else.

Owen turned about and started along the winding path that would serve him along his morning rounds, leaving Jeremiah to continue his vigil. He would stop at each dwelling along the way, checking on the status of each of the residents of the yard.

Paula was an average-sized pig, not awfully large, not too small. She was snuffling about her own small yard just now, in front of the rustic dwelling that was her home. The little plot, bordering the path, was covered in a thin layer of straw.

As with all the small, individual animal yards, all were open to the winding path.

"Good morning, Paula," said Owen, standing tall on the path.

"Good morning to you, Owen." Paula moved nearer the path, stopped. "What is the word?"

"Nothing as yet, I'm afraid."

"I see, I see," she said, nodding slowly and frowning. "Well, soon I am sure."

"No doubt." Owen looked to Paula's dwelling, built sturdy of two-by-fours and cedar boards, intentionally given to look rustic, as were most of the animal homes. "And how are your babies, Paula?"

Paula glanced back at her home. She gave a pleasant snort, a nod, and looked back to Owen.

"Quite well, quite well," she said. "Just about ready to be out on their own."

"And we are all looking forward to that day," said Owen. Another glance to the dwelling, again to Paula. "Is there anything that you need? Anything that I can do?"

"No, no. I do not think so."

Owen sensed Paula's anxiety regarding Mother's absence. It was something they all felt, to be sure.

"Not to worry, Paula," he said, a rather weak attempt at reassurance. "I am certain that all will be well. Mother will return at any moment. In the meantime, the yard will provide."

Most of the animals did have some minimal rations yet remaining to them, and there was a considerable amount of edible vegetation throughout the yard.

"Of course, of course," said Paula. "Thank you."

"Yes. Well," said Owen. "I should continue on then. I have my rounds to complete."

"Of course," said Paula. "Later then."

Owen gave a final nod and continued along the path. His next stop was the home of the pair of pygmy goats, sisters Minnie and Millie. The goat yard was much the same as that of Paula the pig, and the dwelling was much same size as Paula's, if perhaps a bit taller.

The sister goats were nowhere to be seen at the moment, were already out and about.

The path continued on then alongside a small pond. There was a tiny island in the heart of the pond, and there was a small dwelling on the island. The dwelling was the home of a pair of ducks, a married couple named Lloyd and Karen.

They stood now in front of their dwelling, looking across the pond at Owen.

"Owen, my friend," said Lloyd. He took a step nearer. "And how are things?"

"Much the same, Lloyd," said Owen. *For better or for worse...* he thought to himself.

"No news, then?" asked Karen, stepping up beside Lloyd.

"Not as yet, Karen," said Owen. "Soon, I am sure."

"We can but hope," Karen sighed.

"All is well with you?" asked Owen. "Is there anything that you need?"

"A visit from Mother would be nice," said Lloyd. "Not that we don't appreciate the presence of yourself."

"I'll see what I can do," said Owen, giving a departing nod to the couple.

Owen continued on his rounds. He found the rabbit hutch empty, as he expected. Harmony and her two sisters were always early risers and were no doubt out munching on nearby vegetation.

A side trail departed the main path to the left a short way ahead, just before the bend in the main path. This side path disappeared around behind a large fern and led to the back corner of the yard and a small cemetery there. This was where Mother laid to rest the remains of those *no longer here*, placing handmade markers at each grave.

Owen seldom visited the cemetery. He did not do so now, passing it by and continuing along the main trail.

A Canadian goose was sitting peacefully in the tiny yard in front of his dwelling, a small, domelike structure. Nathan the goose had been a rescue animal, taken in by Mother several years earlier. He had been found with a damaged wing and had been having a difficult time in the wild. Quite old now, he was doing well enough in the yard, but everyone suspected that he would soon be *no longer here*, his remains to be taken to the cemetery.

"Good morning to you, my friend," said Owen. He took a single step off the path and settled down just inside Nathan's yard. He often spent a few minutes visiting with Nathan during his morning rounds.

"And to you," said Nathan, giving an easy nod.

"And how are you holding up this day?"

"Well enough, well enough," said Nathan. He managed to scoot a bit nearer to Owen without actually rising. He did not ask about Mother. If there had been word, Owen would have begun their morning chat with such.

Their continuing exchange was kept light, consisting mostly of innocent gossip regarding the latest goings-on of their fellow yard residents. Owen rose up reluctantly after several minutes, gave his wings a gentle shaking and then bid Nathan farewell.

Jeremiah's dwelling was set back only a short distance from the main path. The tortoise's home was constructed from a collection of flat stones, forming a safe, secure structure.

It was empty now, of course, and Owen continued on past.

He visited the hen house next, a dwelling just large enough for the row of six nests belonging to the Council of Hens. The structure sat upon short legs beside the clearing known as the Gathering Place, where the residents of the yard often got together and spent much of the day.

Esther, the head hen, was settled on the horizontal perch pole set before the hen house. She calmly eyed the approaching Owen while simultaneously observing the other hens in her charge as they scratched about for seed, grit and small insects.

"Owen," sighed Esther.

"Esther," Owen stated.

They got along well enough, but they weren't what anyone would consider friends. Esther considered Owen to be quite full of himself, and Owen thought Esther to be overly snooty.

Still, they each considered the other to be necessary to the yard, and so they put up with one another.

"Any thoughts?" asked Esther, just to be polite.

"On what we do if...?" Owen began the thought. "I choose not to assume the worst just yet, Esther."

"No assumptions, Owen. Options, however..."

Owen had no options to offer beyond continuing as they were, relying on what the yard had to offer. Options, however, were no doubt at the top of the agenda of the daily meeting of the Council of Hens.

Owen gave a silent sigh.

A large gray squirrel of the species Western Gray appeared along the top of the back fence. He took a moment to steady himself, looked briefly about then before shifting position and scampering down the fence and to the ground. He worked his way to the path, then casually took the path in stops and starts, passing the yard's animal dwellings along the way, glancing briefly in the direction of each as he went by.

His name was Mister Smythe, and he had been making regular visits to the yard for several months. Mother had given him his name on his third visit, upon first seeing him and welcoming him to the neighborhood. She had first considered naming him Mister Smith, but that didn't quite fit. She was very careful when it came to selecting exactly the right name for each of her children, and no, Smith wasn't right. Smythe... Mister Smythe... was exactly right.

He passed through the Gathering Place, acknowledging the clucking hens, and continued on to the clearing before the back porch of Mother's dwelling. Seeing the tortoise there, he sat beside Jeremiah and studied the back door.

"Hello, Jeremiah," he said, eyes on the door.

"Mister Smythe," said Jeremiah, a slight nod.

"Hmmm," said Mister Smythe. "No sign of Mother, then?"

"I'm afraid not."

"Oh, dear." Mister Smythe settled in. He was in no real hurry to be on his way, and in any case it would have been rude for him to simply leave.

Jeremiah gave a slow side-glance to the squirrel, continued standing his vigil.

Chapter Two

The day drifted slowly and quietly from morning into afternoon.

Owen was midway along his afternoon rounds. He was sitting quietly with Nathan, neither of them speaking. Nathan looked very tired, his eyes half-closed, his breathing shallow.

Nathan liked that Owen was with him just now. It felt comfortable for his friend to be here.

And the afternoon passed.

Many of the residents of the yard were in the Gathering Place, gathered together now in several small groups. Conversations were mostly about Mother's absence.

"What if... what if Mother is *no longer here*?" asked Paula, the mama pig. She looked from Millie to Minnie, the sister pygmy goats. She looked then back in the direction of her dwelling, to where her little ones slept, their midday naps. "What will come of my babies?"

"They have you, Paula," said Millie with a sharp nod of the head. "Your babies will be fine."

Paula gave a noisy sigh at that; her frown remained, her concern unabated.

There were similar conversations going on all about the Gathering Place. There was some concern about what would happen when the food ran out, of course, but most of the discussions were growing increasingly sad rather than worried.

All the residents of the yard cared very much for Mother.

Let her not be *no longer here.*

Owen appeared in the clearing then, looking quite down, gloomy.

Lloyd and Karen, the pair of ducks, turned about together and looked to Owen.

"What is it, Owen?" asked Lloyd.

"Nathan," said Owen simply.

"The Old One?" asked Karen. Others in the clearing moved nearer.

"The Old One, yes," said Owen, heavily, glumly. "I fear that Nathan will soon be *no longer here.*"

The Gathering Place immediately fell silent at that, a melancholy darkness settling over the clearing. None said it aloud, but many thought to themselves...

Will the Old One soon be with Mother?

Reggie was on his final neighborhood explore of the day. He sat high on his perch in the tree near The Woman's yard, looking down on the goings-on below. He could see the group of hens were gathered together, apparently in the midst of one of their group meetings.

Curious. The chickens usually held their little get-togethers in the late morning.

Reggie quietly observed for a few moments, looked about then at the goings-on that were going on elsewhere in the yard. He moved on then.

The afternoon explore must continue.

An unscheduled meeting of the Council of Hens. Esther spoke briefly to the question of Nathan, whom most believed would soon be no longer here. Adjustments would have to be made as to what would happen after he was no longer here.

Mother usually dealt with the what-next.

This brought to the discussion the matter at the forefront of the minds of most in the Council.

Ruby, the most outspoken of the hens, was quite concerned that there had been no sign of Mother.

"Yes, yes..." Fay said meekly to that. Fay, gentle, unassuming.

Others spoke up then, polite yet insistent, each voicing their own apprehensions. Beatrice, Blanche, Mabel...

"Of course, of course," Esther stated firmly. "Mother or no, we must not ignore our other concerns."

Ruby clucked and bobbed her head up and down, clucked again.

"We cannot continue with this uncertainty," she said. "Someone must go into Mother's dwelling, look for signs, learn more."

A heavy silence fell over the group for several long moments.

"You don't think..." Fay's thought faded.

"I do not think one way or another," stated Esther. "Ruby is correct. There are no answers in the yard. They must be sought for elsewhere."

Chapter Three

Millie and Minnie drank from the pond, then slowly worked their way toward the fence running along the side of the yard, stopping here and there to munch a leaf or two from one shrub or another. They occasionally grazed on wild grass, though being pygmy goats they targeted only the leafiest fronds of such. They reached the row of low bushes that grew along the fence and began pulling down and munching on leaves.

Much more to their liking.

This was nothing new for the sisters. This was how they spent most of their mornings. The difference on this particular morning was that they had finished the last of the food they had been carefully rationing. If Mother failed to make an appearance soon, shrub leaves and leafy grass would be their entire diet.

They heard then a scratching, scraping sound, this followed by low, gruffy growling.

They stepped back from the bush they had been munching on and looked down the fence line.

A medium-sized, thick muscled dog, part bulldog, mostly mutt, was just scrambling up from under the fence, coming from the yard next door. He shook off the dirt, gave off a low ruff sound and looked at the pair of pygmy goats.

Neither Millie nor Minnie seemed particularly frightened; nor were they surprised.

The dog gave another ruff sound, tilted his head, studied the goats. He shook himself a second time.

The dog's name was Max. This was the name given him by his owners, the human next-door neighbors. Despite appearances, Max was a friendly sort. He was also an occasional visitor to Mrs. Weddington's yard.

Despite such frequent visits however, Max's vocabulary seemed limited to ruffs and gruffy arfs and curious, questioning barks.

He took a few steps nearer the sister goats, let out a pair of ruffs, then turned and loped off to visit others of the yard.

Millie and Minnie returned to their leaf munching.

Max continued along the path. He hadn't gone more than a few paces when he slowed, stopped. He had sensed something. There had come a tingling along the back of his neck.

He sat, looked over at the fence, some four long strides away.

A large cat was lounging on the top of the fence, his front legs crossed, his chin resting on his paws. He was looking in the general direction of Max without giving the appearance of looking in the direction of Max.

Max gave a single, low, grumbling harrumph in the cat's general direction.

The cat responded with a barely perceptible twitch of one ear. Nothing more.

Mother had made several attempts at befriending the cat in the past, whom she had named Oliver, but the cat had not been the friendliest of guests. It had made a number of threats against most of the residents of the yard.

In the end, Mother had been forced to send the cat on its way, this despite Mother's strong desire to welcome all critters into her world; witness the squirrel Mister Smythe, the neighbor dog Max, the adoption of Nathan the goose; there was even that strange bird Reggie, who visited daily while seldom actually landing in the yard.

Now, after all this time, the cat had returned.

Oliver let out a long, tired yawn, casually rose up then onto all fours. He stretched, oh so slowly, and glanced calmly over at Max. After ensuring that any who might be watching could see that he wasn't in the least bit concerned, he hopped from the fence down into the neighbor's yard.

Max stood then, gave a proud, satisfied gruff and continued on his way.

The duck couple Lloyd and Karen arrived in the clearing, the word having gone out that there was to be a Gathering Place meeting. They waddled slowly toward others already gathering there.

The hens were clustered together, as they most often were, always at the direction of Esther, Head Hen. The three rabbits had settled themselves side-by-side off to their left, where they waited patiently, silently, their noses twitching.

Paula was there. She was concerned at leaving her babies alone for any length of time, but sensed the meeting to be important.

The sister goats arrived then, coming from another path. They acknowledged the others in the clearing as they entered, looking about at those present. There was no sign of Jeremiah, but that was to be expected. He would no doubt be vigilantly standing his watch before the back porch.

"Owen?" asked Millie and Minnie, almost simultaneously.

"He is with The Old One," said Lloyd. He and Karen had passed the turkey on their way to the clearing. Owen had been sitting with Nathan.

"Shall we begin, then?" prompted Paula.

"Yes," said Millie.

"Is there news of Mother?" added Minnie.

"I am afraid not," said Esther.

"The purpose of this meeting then?" asked Paula, urging.

"Of course. Of course," said Esther, giving her wings a light flutter, fluffing her down feathers.

"And so?" prompted Lloyd.

"Very well," said Esther. "Per our earlier meeting of the Council of Hens, it has been determined that we must go into Mother's dwelling. We must look for clues as to what may have happened to Mother."

An uncomfortable shuddering drifted across all gathered in the clearing.

Mother is no longer here...

"I make no assumptions as to what we might find," said Esther. "As there are no answers to be found in the yard, we must look elsewhere."

Mother is no longer here...

"Enter Mother's dwelling?" asked Lloyd. "How do we do that?"

"Yes," said Karen. "Who of us could possibly—"

"Mister Smythe," Esther stated calmly.

Everyone slowly shifted their attention to the large, gray squirrel that was sitting at the edge of the clearing, just in front of a cluster of bushes. Mister Smythe nervously drummed his clawed front toes together. He watched then as Millie turned and stepped nearer, her sister Minnie following beside her. They stopped a pace before the squirrel.

"Mister Smythe is more a daily visitor than full-time resident of the yard," said Millie, half-tilting her head and giving the squirrel a steady gaze.

"A friend, nonetheless," said Minnie.

"Yes. Yes, I agree," said Millie. She straightened her head and looked down upon the squirrel. "Would you be willing to take on such a task, Mister Smythe?"

"He must," Esther said firmly, stepping up and positioning herself between the two goats. Others in the clearing moved nearer, coming up behind the goats and Esther. "Who else among us is capable?"

"Anything for Mother, of course," said Mister Smythe, continuing to drum his front toes together. "How to do so, however..."

He had found his way into the attic of Mother's dwelling some time past, but never a way into the house itself.

"The window," said Karen.

"Yes, the window," said Lloyd.

The three rabbits, sitting one beside the other, all nodded in unison.

"The window?" asked Esther.

Karen shifted position, looked in the direction of the dwelling beyond the clearing, beyond the band of thick vegetation between clearing and dwelling.

"Just around the corner of Mother's dwelling," she said. "A small window high in the wall."

"The window is always open," said Lloyd. "Just a tad. Perhaps it is locked so."

"Just wide enough for Mister Smythe."

All again turned about to look at the critter sitting tall just at the edge of the clearing.

"I could give it a try," he said at last.

"Good for you," said Esther.

All gave their assent. Mister Smythe would enter the dwelling and search for evidence as to what may have happened to Mother. Perhaps determine whether Mother was still here...

Or *is no longer here...*

A sense of a change then, of something not quite right then. A hush fell over the scene as all turned slowly about. They watched Owen come solemnly into the clearing, stopping several paces from group.

He stood silent.

"What is it, Owen?" asked Esther.

"Nathan," said Owen after a long pause. "Nathan. Nathan is no longer here."

Chapter Four

The Council of Hens were clustered together at the edge of the clearing, clucking away anxiously, their words barely understandable; *what to do, what to do.*

The three rabbits had scooted all the nearer each other, noses twitching, uncertain what to say regarding the news. They had seen little of Nathan of late, seldom traveling that far along the path, but they had liked him very much all the same.

There was no sign of Owen. Having imparted his sad news, he had continued solemnly on his way.

"What are we to do?" asked Millie.

"Mother needs to be here," said Minnie.

The goat couple nodded. The rabbits tilted their heads slightly, temporarily stopped their twitching.

Yes. Mother. It was Mother who prepared a place for remains in the cemetery. When one was no longer here, it was Mother who took care of everything.

"What if Mother is with Nathan?" asked Lloyd.

"She isn't," said Karen, uncertainly, slowly shaking her head. "I know that she isn't."

Esther stepped away from the other hens.

"We can't know one way or the other," she stated firmly. "We know only that Mother is not with us at the moment and that we must take care of this ourselves."

"Yes. Yes, I agree," said Lloyd at last. He shifted his weight from one foot to the other. He looked from his wife Karen to Esther. "How are we to do that?"

All were silent for several long moments.

Harmony, leader of the rabbits, looked from one to the other of her sisters, then edged forward.

"We will prepare a place in the cemetery," she said.

"You can do this?" asked Millie.

Harmony held her front paws up, gave a single sharp nod. Her sisters scooted up beside her. Each held up their front paws.

"Very good," said Esther. She looked then to Millie and Minnie. She waited for some sign from the pair of goats.

Nothing at first. Not for some long moments.

Finally then, Millie gave a grudging nod.

"Very well," she said, a side-glance to Minnie, then a general glance about at the others in the clearing. "We will take the remains to the cemetery."

"Very good," said Esther, a second time.

Mister Smythe, sitting on his rump, had silently watched this all from the far edge of the clearing. He dropped down onto all fours now and followed after Owen. Coming into the back porch clearing, he waited politely several paces behind Owen and Jeremiah as the turkey broke the news of Nathan to the tortoise. Jeremiah had been expecting it, of course, they all had. That didn't make it any easier to hear.

"We need Mother," said Jeremiah.

"I know that," said Owen. "Mother isn't here."

They were quiet then.

Mister Smythe came forward, settled in beside his friends.

"Nathan is to be seen to," he stated. "Arrangements are already being made. Preparations will begin soon."

Owen and Jeremiah gave silent acknowledgment at that. Jeremiah continued to focus on the back door of Mother's dwelling.

What if Mother is gone forever?

Despite his unbidden fears, Jeremiah refused to speak such thoughts aloud. He was not ready to go that far. Not yet.

"We need Mother," he stated simply, again.

"I have no doubt we will learn something soon," said Mister Smythe. He looked to the house. His own thoughts went to his soon to be explore. "Very soon."

Owen was standing alongside the main path, wispy rays of the afternoon sun reaching through the trees and splaying all about the yard, creating shadows and sunlight.

Looking up the path, Owen watched the hens, just starting from the main trail to the cemetery side-trail, disappearing around the large fern. Turning to look to his left then, he watched Jeremiah coming up the trail just as fast as he was able, eventually reaching the turkey.

"I hope they'll wait, Owen," said the tortoise. "Do you expect they'll wait?"

"Of course they'll wait," said Owen. "Don't you worry on that, Jeremiah."

"I really should have started earlier." Jeremiah gave a tired shake of the head as he continued on his way.

"They'll wait," Owen called after him, a confident nod of his own. He watched after the tortoise a few moments more, shook his head and looked again then to his left.

If he leaned his head back he could just make out Paula's yard. She had already told Owen that she wouldn't be able to make the ceremony, but he had nonetheless hoped.

She had yet to make an appearance.

He saw then Lloyd and Karen step out onto the path. The duck couple shuffled quickly toward Owen. They nodded in silent greeting as they passed, soon reaching and then passing Jeremiah on their way to the cemetery side-trail, disappearing around the fern.

That would be it then. The others were already at the cemetery.

Owen gave a final glance back to Paula's yard, then stepped out onto the path and started toward the cemetery. He reached Jeremiah, who was just turning into the side-trail. The two of them silently continued on together. Entering the cemetery grounds, they approached the other residents of the yard, all gathered around a small mound of recently turned soil.

Millie and Minnie, the goats who had brought Nathan's remains, stood side-by-side at the far end of the mound. Harmony and her sister rabbits, who had prepared the grave and then filled it in again afterward, sat along one side of the mound.

The hens and the pair of ducks were just settling in opposite the rabbits.

Jeremiah and Owen approached the near end of the mound.

All were silent. The silence seemed to last a very long time.

An uncomfortable sigh from Lloyd then, looking down at the grave mound.

"Words, then?" he asked.

"Mother," Karen mumbled. *Mother always said the words...*

"Mother isn't here," said Lloyd, looking up from the grave, glancing about at those gathered.

There was more silence.

"Nathan was a gentle soul," said Jeremiah.

A few nods of agreement from several of those gathered.

"He was the kindest of us," said Esther, the first words from the hens.

More nods of agreement.

Again, silence, all looking down at the grave mound.

"The grave is unfinished," said Millie. "Mother needs to make the marker."

"Mother isn't here," Lloyd said, quietly, a second time.

"What if Mother is with the Old One?" asked Millie, indicating Nathan's grave.

There was a final, very long quiet.

"Nathan was my friend," said Owen.

Chapter Five

Most of the residents of the yard had gathered before the wall of the Mother's dwelling, were quietly watching Mister Smythe as he walked along the base, studying the wall, determining the best approach.

Owen stood at the back of the group, some feet behind the others, watching Mister Smythe as he also watched those who were watching the squirrel.

Paula stepped up beside Owen. She looked at the small window that was set high in the wall.

"Quite a climb," she said quietly to Owen. "Difficult."

They watched as Owen reached out and touched the wall's rough surface, testing the gripability.

"He can do it," said Owen.

"Sure, sure." Paula looked off to one side then, behind her then. "I need to get back to my babies."

"Of course. Responsibilities," Owen stated matter-of-factly. He understood responsibility. "I'll let you know what comes of Mister Smythe's investigation."

Paula thanked Owen, hesitating.

Owen gave a short nod in reply, watched side-glance as Paula finally started away. He focused fully then on Mister Smythe, who was now beginning his shaky, scrambling ascent up the wall. He slipped several times, managing each time to regain his grip.

He finally reached the narrow sill, glanced down at those watching below. He gave a slight nod and then, after first attempting and failing to push the window open further, turned and squeezed through the narrow opening.

Once inside, he looked back at the window, noticed a stick set in the window slide. This explained why the window wouldn't open more than a few inches.

He looked out at the room before him. It appeared to be a crafts room of sorts. Counters ran along several walls, three tall stools set before them. There were crafting materials on the counters, on shelves, in boxes on the floor.

Cluttered, yet at the same time neat and organized.

And all was very quiet.

Mister Smythe hopped from the sill down onto the counter. He quickly scurried several feet and then jumped down onto the nearest stool and then down onto the floor.

He moved cautiously to the open door, paused and peeked out into the hallway.

Quiet. Shadowed. The only light came from windows in the other rooms off the hallway.

It was all rather unsettling.

Mister Smythe walked down the hall, staying close to the wall. He passed several doorways, looking quickly into each as he scurried past.

Each room was clean, neat, organized.

Such was Mother.

The hallway emptied into the large main room. It appeared at first as the rest of the dwelling, clean and organized, but as he crossed the room toward a wide archway opening, Mister Smythe hesitated and looked back into the room.

It appeared that some of the furniture had been pushed aside, creating a clear path from the archway that he was approaching across to the front foyer opposite.

Curious.

Mister Smythe continued on then through the archway and into another room.

The kitchen, though of course he did not know that was what it was called.

There were strange smells here. Not pleasant.

Food. Old food.

He hurried over to a chair, hopped onto the chair and then up onto a small table. From there, he leapt onto a counter. From here he could see most of the room.

Large appliances were set between cabinets. Counter-top appliances were sitting on the counters. There was a large double sink. Several packages were set out on one of the counters. On the table behind him, a plate with old food, a fork and knife beside the plate, a glass with something smelly inside.

Not at all like the rest of the dwelling.

This was not right.

Mister Smythe sat back on his haunches, held his front paws out before him. His nose twitched nervously.

This was not right at all.

A large group had clustered around Mister Smythe in the center of the Gathering Place clearing. They listened as he detailed his explore as fully as he was able, adding his own insights when he thought it would be helpful.

He finished then, and those who were gathered around him were very quiet for several long moments.

"Well, to the positive," said Karen, at last, "not finding Mother means that she is not *no longer here*. Is that not right?"

Her husband Lloyd silently agreed, the pair of ducks giving slow, easy nods.

"I'm afraid that is not necessarily so, Karen," countered Esther, sadly. "She may be no longer here somewhere else."

"Ah, yes," sighed Karen. "Of course."

The group again fell silent, each considering all that they had heard.

"It would not be like Mother to leave food on the table to grow old," said Minnie then.

Minnie's sister Millie silently agreed, the two goats giving slow, easy nods.

"She left in a hurry," Owen stated firmly. "Either on her own or perhaps taken."

"Oh my," said several of the group.

"And the furniture in the main room," said Esther. "Pushed aside, creating a path from the bad food room to the front door of Mother's dwelling. What is that about?"

Again, all fell silent. They all had their unspoken suspicions.

Jeremiah quietly moved away from the others, started across the clearing.

It was time for him to return to his watch at the back porch.

Mother will return.

Mother will care for her children.

Oliver stopped, dropped down onto his belly, front paws extended.

Up ahead along the path, six piglets were playing in the small yard just off to the right. Oliver quietly watched as they wrestled with one another, rolling about happily, stopping occasionally to dig at the ground with their sharp little hooves, noisily burying their snouts into the rich mulch.

The cat crept forward, nearer, nearer, legs trembling slightly. Still too far away to pounce, Oliver suddenly found himself face to face with a much larger pig.

Paula.

There had been dealings with Paula in the past and they had never ended well. At the very least, they could have gone better.

Oliver slowly lifted himself up, straightened and, doing his best to demonstrate his total lack of concern, continued on his way, albeit as far to the left along the trail as he could manage. Mama pig eyed Oliver all the while, always facing the cat, shifting her weight and ready to strike at the slightest indication of danger to her babies.

Fine. I didn't really want the piglets anyway.

Tail raised high, strutting along the path, Oliver rounded the bend.

He could hear the clucking long before he saw them.

Ah... better...

Oliver moved off the trail, crept through the brush and settled in at the edge of the clearing. The hens were off to his left in the clearing, were scratching and pecking at the mulchy ground, were slowly working their way in his direction.

Oliver waited.

Esther, the head hen, watched her charge from nearby, occasionally giving the ground a distracted scratch of her own.

Oliver crept ever-so-slightly forward. A hesitant twitch.

Patience, patience...

The hens continued to scratch their way nearer, nearer.

Now...

Oliver leapt into the clearing, landed, immediately pushed off his back feet, reaching out with his front paws and grasping onto the nearest chicken.

Fay.

She cried out, wings and legs flailing. The other hens scattered in a panic, wings aflutter.

All but Esther. Esther rushed forward, head down, jumping at the last and pushing her claws forward.

Fay and Oliver and Esther, a swirling cloud of feathers and fur and claws. Fay continued crying out in fear, Oliver screeching in pain, Esther screaming in rage.

Seeming out of nowhere then, Owen rushed into the clearing, half flying, half at a dead run. A final jump and his claws buried into Oliver's back.

Fay found herself suddenly free and she fluttered hurriedly away. It took a bit more time and effort for Esther to work herself free of the cat. She stepped back, head down and beak pushed threateningly forward, hissing.

Only then did Owen release himself from the cat and jump aside. He spread his wings wide, angrily fanned and fluttered his tail.

He jumped a step toward the cat.

Oliver hurried out of the clearing with as much dignity as he could muster. It wasn't much, but he managed to walk with his head held high. He hadn't gone more than a few yards when he began to hear a heavy thumping sound coming from behind him, drawing nearer and nearer. Half-turning his head, he saw Max, the dog's lips pulled back and teeth bared, rushing toward him, big, meaty paws pounding along the path... *thump, thump, thump-thump, thump.*

Oliver faced full forward and started off as fast as he could. Rounding the bend, he jumped into the brush and, leaping pell-mell, bounded toward the fence. He jumped, claws scraping at the wood. He didn't quite reach the top of the fence and slid back to the ground.

He could hear Max tearing through the brush, was almost upon him. Running further along the fenceline, he jumped up onto a low, rotting stump and leaped up to the top of the fence. All four paws scrambled and scraped to keep him from losing his balance and falling back into the slobbering jaws of death.

Composure quickly returned.

He sat then on his rear haunches, looked down at the dog. Max had his front paws on the top of the stump, was growling low, mixing in an occasional gruffy ruff.

Oliver took a moment more to calmly lick his front paws. He gave the dog a last, dismissive glance and rose up, hopped from the fence and dropped into the neighbor's yard.

Chapter Six

Morning.

Reggie was on his first neighborhood explore of the day. Arriving at his first regular stop of the morning, he came in low over The Woman's dwelling, gliding above the rooftop then out over the yard. He spread his wings wide and drifted upward. He rose above the perch, hung there a moment, then settled down onto the branch. The treetop swayed from side to side and Reggie fluttered his wings to maintain his balance.

All calm, then. He brought his wings in.

He was facing the wrong direction.

Okay, all is not lost.

He shifted about, turning, turning, adjusting the position of his feet, maintaining a grip on the branch.

That was not going to work.

He spread his wings again, beat them several times and lifted himself from the branch perch. Rising upward, Reggie drifted outward, slowly circled the above yard. Coming back around then, he approached the tree from the other direction. Landing a second time on his perch, the treetop swayed, again, and he fluttered his wings to maintain his balance.

All settled then, all calm again, Reggie brought his wings in.

Better now.

Reggie began his observation of the yard below.

§

Jeremiah could hear sounds coming from inside Mother's dwelling.

Yes, there was movement on the other side of the back door.

Could it be Mother?

Jeremiah anxiously watched and waited.

A woman stepped out the door and onto the porch. She was carrying a basket of fruit and vegetables, diced and sliced.

No. It was not Mother. But Jeremiah recognized her from a number of previous visits. Mother referred to her as Emma; she was Mother's niece.

Emma walked to the edge of the porch, to the top of the steps. She held the basket to one side as she took the steps down to the ground. She stopped briefly then as she looked about the yard, smiling briefly down at Jeremiah.

Word was already spreading throughout the yard. Animals began approaching, albeit cautiously, for the moment keeping their distance.

"Hello, little ones," she said, giving a broad smile to the residents of the yard. If her aunt was to be believed, and Emma did believe her, the gathering critters actually understood her words, though she, and her aunt, only heard animal sounds in response.

"It's just me, I'm afraid," she continued. "Remember me? Of course you do."

Emma had been to the yard a number of times, having visited her aunt many times, going back to when she was much younger. She had helped her aunt feed and care for the residents of the yard many times, and so knew where everything was and what needed doing.

She started toward the food shed, speaking as she walked.

"Your Mother asked me to take care of you while she's away," she said. "Don't you worry though, little ones. She'll be with you again soon."

And with that she heard what she took to be excited, happy animal sounds from most of the critters that were gathering now nearer around her.

Animal Talk, her aunt called it.

"You got that, huh?" she asked, another broad smile. Reaching the food shed, she opened the door and went inside. She set the basket of fruit and vegetables on a small table, picked up a serving pan and went to the wall of shelves and drawers. This was where the assorted animal foods were kept; specific foods for each of Auntie's critters.

She spent the next hour and then some looking after her aunt's children, jabbering away throughout the morning, listening to their happy Animal Talk in answer.

With her chores completed, Emma closed up the food shed and started back to the house. She slowed as she approached the porch. Hesitating a moment, she stopped and turned about, sat on the edge of the porch. She rested her feet on the bottom step, placed her elbows on her knees and clasped her hands. She looked out across the clearing, smiled solemnly as she watched the menagerie of animals come cautiously nearer.

In one sense or another, I know you understand me. Emotions, certainly. Thoughts? Maybe actual words?

"Oh, little ones," she said, barely more than a sigh. The critters crept ever nearer, stopped then, watched Emma the niece, and waited.

The turkey waddled another step nearer, stopped, studied.

It was his duty.

Emma gave another broad grin.

"It's Owen, isn't it?" she asked. "You tough old bird."

Owen tilted his head slightly to one side, straightened again. Proud.

"You know," Emma continued. "Auntie's a tough old bird. Your Mother."

Emma sat there, on the edge of the porch, no longer in any real hurry to leave. She talked to her aunt's children.

They listened to Emma the niece, and were, at least for the moment, content.

§

Lloyd was gliding oh-so-slowly about in their duck pond, creating barely a ripple on the water's smooth surface. He drifted over toward the tiny island, eased to a stop a few feet from the shore. He waited, watched as Karen waddled from their shelter to the shore and slipped into the water. Together then, they drifted from the island. They quietly took in the pleasant morning, a light, misty gray that was soon to clear to another sunny day.

If they noticed Owen approaching, coming along the path, they chose not to acknowledge the turkey. They continued to drift, in no particular direction, eyes closed.

Not wanting to disturb the couple, who were clearly enjoying the morning, Owen walked past without speaking.

Rounding the next bend, he came to a sudden stop. He tilted his head a bit to the left and took in the scene.

Paula was walking along the path, coming slowly towards him. Following along behind her walked her babies, out and about for the first time.

Owen stepped aside, off the trail, as Paula neared.

"Good morning, Owen," said the mama pig, passing.

"Paula," said Owen with a nod.

Paula continued past, her babies strutting proudly in line behind her.

Owen stepped back onto the path then, watched the little parade as it continued round the bend. He continued on his rounds then, worked his way toward the back of the yard and then the next bend in the trail. He slowed slightly, hesitating briefly, when he saw the cat straddled along the top of the back fence. From here the fence was a number of long strides distant.

Oliver made no move, chin resting on his folded front paws. Owen gave the cat a sharp nod of the head, a quiet snort.

Oliver blinked, once, twice, gave a long breath, as if a silent acknowledgement that for now the yard was out of bounds, off limits to him.

The top of the back fence, however, was allowable.

Owen gave it a thought.

Very well.

Owen gave the cat a final nod and continued on his way.

Coming around the last bend, a shadow drifted across the path several feet in front of him. Glancing up, Owen saw the large raven gliding overhead. He stepped to one side to better watch as Reggie approached his tree, fluttered his wings as he settled onto his perch.

Yes.

It was a pleasant morning indeed.

Chapter Seven

It was a day gone by since Emma's visit. Another day without Mother.

Jeremiah watched the back door open.

Could this be it? Jeremiah lifted himself up, anxiously pushed himself forward on his short, stubby legs.

Yes? Yes?

He saw then Mother step out onto the porch. She hesitated a moment, then walked slowly forward. She was holding a strange stick in one hand, leaning on it, seemed to be using it as a third leg.

She continued out and stood at the top of the steps.

Mrs. Weddington was in her sixties. She was a tall woman, full-figured, dressed now in loose blouse and pants, wearing the familiar boots she always wore when visiting her children. Her thick, salt-and-pepper hair hung to her shoulders.

She appeared a bit weary to Jeremiah, but otherwise well enough.

She looked down at the tortoise, gave him a loving smile.

"My dear Jeremiah," she said. She took the steps, struggled as she managed to sit on the bottom step. She set the strange stick aside, reached her hand out then and called softly. "Come to me, little one."

Jeremiah quickly strode the last few feet to Mother. She reached out and scratched under his chin.

"How have you been, little one? I have certainly missed you."

Jeremiah managed a few clicks and twitters. This brought another broad smile to Mother.

"Well, I am home now," she said. "Don't you worry now. I won't be leaving you again any time soon."

As she talked with Jeremiah, others of the yard came into the clearing, slowly at first, quickly then as they realized that it was indeed Mother. Hurrying to gather near, they began calling excited to her.

Mother! Mother! So glad to see you! So glad you are still here!

So glad you are not no longer here!

Mother listened to her children, hearing the chirps and chitters and titters of their animal talk, yet somehow sensing their words and their thoughts. Her own words gave them comfort and warmth. She talked of how much she missed them, missed them all so very, very much, how happy she was to be home.

After a time then, she leaned forward and struggled to her feet, using that strange stick to balance herself.

"Make way, children," she said. She stepped away from the steps and started across the clearing, her walking stick in hand. "Let us see what we have for you today. Shall we?"

Reggie, sitting on his perch high atop the tree, quickly regained his footing after pushing back against a sudden breeze. He watched The Woman as she walked across the clearing. Many of the yard's critters were hovering all about her, scurrying about underfoot as she worked her way to one of the sheds. He could just barely make out The Woman laughing lightly, trying her best to avoid stepping on any of them, to not trip over them.

Early afternoon, Owen was taking a break from his midday rounds, was sitting quietly now with Jeremiah. It had been quite a morning, what with Mother's return, and most in the yard were spending the afternoon relaxing, chattering quietly with one another, speaking of life and Mother and, well, again... *of life.*

Life in the yard was good. Very good. Life with their fellows, with good friends.

And Mother had returned.

Mother was <u>not</u> *no longer here.*

Esther came into the clearing, came up beside Owen and Jeremiah. She fluffed her wings several times, shifted her body one way and then the other. She settled herself down and squatted then beside the turkey and the tortoise.

Owen and Jeremiah each glanced aside at the hen, said nothing.

Esther lifted herself up, adjusted her wings, settled down again.

"Shouldn't you be going about on your rounds?" she asked Owen.

"I'm thinking that later will be soon enough," he answered after a moment.

This brought a light cluck and a brief nod of the head from Esther.

All three were quiet again; Jeremiah, Esther, Owen.

After some long moments the silence began to grow a bit less comfortable.

"And how are the ladies?" asked Owen of the other hens. The Council of Hens.

"They're resting," she answered. "Taking a siesta."

"Siesta," mumbled Owen. "I see."

"It was an exhausting day," said Jeremiah, facing forward, eyes half-closed.

"A most agreeable one," said Esther.

Owen and Jeremiah gave silent assent.

A small, thin cloud, high in the blue sky, drifted slowly over. It created a shadow that passed across the clearing. It moved on then and the warm sunlight returned.

Owen slowly lifted himself up.

"Perhaps I will take a quick walk around the yard," he said. He had to move slightly to give himself room to stretch his wings. "I should give it all a onceover."

He was gone then. Esther looked side-glance at the space left behind between herself and Jeremiah.

She lifted herself up, shifted to the left, settled back beside Jeremiah.

Chapter Eight

Mother walked carefully amongst the wooden markers to the fresh grave. She bore a very solemn expression. Kneeling, she pushed the newly made marker into place at the head of the grave.

She laid a hand on the grave.

I should have been here with you...

"I am so sorry, Nathan," she said sadly. "I am so, so sorry. I should have been here for you. I should have been with you."

Goodbye, my friend.

She sat back then, rested her hands in her lap. She sat there, beside the grave then, for a very long time. The late afternoon slowly faded to early evening.

Mother finally shifted about and struggled to lift herself up, grasping the cane and using it to push herself to her feet. She wiped moisture from her cheek, tried her best to give a warm farewell smile to her departed friend.

She walked from the cemetery path and onto the yard's main trail. She was all the more dependent on the cane after sitting for so long. A few steps along and she saw the large squirrel sitting tall alongside the trail, waiting for her.

"Ah, there you are, Mister Smythe," she said, struggling to push aside her sorrow. "I missed you this morning."

Mister Smythe stepped out onto the trail, came a little nearer Mother. He hopped and scooted along as Mother started forward again, Mister Smythe chirping and chittering as they walked.

And Mother felt a little better.

Morning in the yard began under a thin fog that drifted along the labyrinth of trails, across the several clearings, the ponds, the handful of animal dwellings. The large raven flew above the mist, landed gently on his perch and struggled to maintain his balance as the treetop swung back and forth.

Reggie shifted position so that he could take in the scene below. The warmth of the morning sun was doing its work and the mist was quickly burning off.

The hens were just beginning to stir, stepping hesitantly down the short ramp from the henhouse to the ground.

The mama pig was already out and about, her babies moving about their small yard, nosing about in the mulch.

The Tortoise had left his dwelling and was just starting down the yard's main trail. It would take him a while to get wherever he was going.

There was no sign of the others just yet; they had yet to stir themselves out of their dwellings.

Ah, well...

Reggie prepared to continue his morning explore, to move on to his next stop.

Down below then, the Turkey was just beginning to make his appearance, began clambering out of his dwelling.

Reggie settled back onto his perch. He would hang around just a few minutes more. He would watch for the rest of the yard to awaken.

End...

www.ingramcontent.com/pod-product-compliance
Lightning Source LLC
Chambersburg PA
CBHW022055170626
46808CB00003B/1475